CARTOON NETWORK

Ed, Edd n Eddy™

LOTS OF LAUGHS

Based on episodes
of ED, EDD N EDDY:
Sir Ed-A-Lot
Who, What, Where, Ed
and *Hot Buttered Ed*
as created by
Danny Antonucci

By Jesse Leon McCann

SCHOLASTIC INC.
New York   Toronto   London   Auckland   Sydney
Mexico City   New Delhi   Hong Kong   Buenos Aires

ISBN 0-439-77942-1

Designed by Joseph Williams

12 11 10 9·8 7 6 5 4 3 2 1   5 6 7 8 9 10/0

Printed in the U.S.A.

First printing, June 2005

1.

In a suburb named Peach Creek, in a neighborhood known as the cul-de-sac (because that's what it was), a boy named Eddy proudly polished a souped-up, cherry-red sports car. He wore a big grin.

Now, Eddy wasn't the most popular kid in the neighborhood. He wasn't always the nicest person and was often greedy. You might even say he had a reputation for being a knucklehead. (In fact, if you make a fist and look at your knuckles, that's sort of what Eddy's head looked like!)

Nevertheless, Eddy knew that he looked pretty cool buffing the sports car, with its four on the floor, tail fins, and overhead cam engine. He didn't know what any of those things were for, but they sounded awesome!

Eddy was just waiting for someone to notice him

and the car. He didn't have to wait very long.

"Hey, Jonny-boy!" Eddy coolly pointed a finger at Jonny 2x4, who was coming his way.

"Hi, Eddy. Nice car!" Jonny smiled as he passed by with his best friend, Plank.

Eddy was pleased with the compliment, even though he considered Jonny a major weirdo. Jonny hung out almost exclusively with Plank. Plank was a piece of wood with a face painted on it. Jonny swore Plank talked to him, even though no one else ever heard anything.

Whatever, thought Eddy. *A compliment is a compliment!*

Speaking of weirdos, Rolf stopped by next.

"Yello, Eddy," Rolf lightly touched the surface of the car, admiring it like it was a precious gem.

Eddy tolerated Rolf, since he was usually good for a few laughs with his strange, foreign ways. Not long ago, Rolf's family came to America from . . . actually, Eddy didn't know *where* Rolf emigrated from. Whatever country it was, they had bizarre customs and ate really gross food.

"May we shop for meat in your fancy car?" Rolf asked, eyes glistening.

Eddy laughed. "Keep dreaming, Rolf." No way was Rolf getting into the car.

Rolf wandered off, and Eddy climbed in behind the steering wheel. Now he was ultra-styling! As luck would have it, Nazz and Kevin strolled by. Nazz was the cutest girl in the neighborhood and Kevin was the most obnoxious bully on the planet. Eddy slowly lowered the tinted window and gave them a little smirk.

"Hi, Nazz," Eddy said casually.

"Wow, Eddy! Cool car!" Nazz said. What a sweetheart she was!

"Hey, dork," Kevin frowned. "Whose car is this, you twerp?"

Leave it to Kevin to be a drag. Eddy closed the window and ended the conversation. Kevin knocked on the window.

Eddy turned the radio up REALLY LOUD. The music was so loud that the car started bouncing up and down on the street. Nazz and Kevin covered their ears and ran away.

Just then, Double-D, one of Eddy's best friends, walked up. "Hey, Eddy. What are you doing?"

Eddy just grinned and pointed to the car.

Double-D and Eddy were members of an exclusive group in the cul-de-sac made up of boys with "Ed" in their names. Double-D's real name was Edd, with two *d*'s. Calling him Double-D made things a whole lot simpler.

Double-D was the smartest of the Eds, not that Eddy would ever admit it to anyone, and he was also the kindest and the most polite.

But Eddy considered himself the leader of the group, the one who came up with all the best ideas. In truth, Eddy had led the Eds into mischief more than once. . . .

Double-D looked the vehicle up and down. "Whose car is this, Eddy?" he asked.

"Beats me," Eddy said.

2.

"Where's Ed?" Eddy asked, throwing the polishing cloth away. He was bored with the car and ready for a new adventure. But before the fun could begin, they would need the third member of their group.

"I called his residence, but there was no answer," Double-D said.

Eddy took off his sunglasses and pointed into the air. "Let's hunt him down!"

They ran to Ed's house and peeked into the basement window. Ed's bedroom was in the basement. It was a mess, filled with trash, spills, junk, and memorabilia from old monster movies. Ed loved old monster movies.

"Do you see him?" Double-D inquired.

"*Whoop!*" Eddy sneaked through the window and looked around. "Nope!"

Eddy loved sneaking.

Double-D followed him in. "Perhaps we should check upstairs."

"I'll bet he's just hiding." Eddy looked under a stuffed chair cushion, revealing even more garbage and a few dead flies.

Double-D snickered and pointed to the bed. There was a shape under the blanket. It looked as if Ed was still asleep. Edd and Eddy glanced at each other with mischievous grins.

"Dog pile!" they cried in unison, jumping heads-first onto the bed.

Clang!

Recoiling from the impact, Edd and Eddy rubbed their sore noggins. Eddy pulled the blanket off. That wasn't Ed! For some reason, Ed had put a car bumper in his bed.

Just then, a loud noise came from upstairs. They gasped. Part of Ed's ceiling came loose and hit Eddy square on the head.

"Let's check upstairs," Eddy suggested. He giggled

as they ran upstairs. This was turning into a game of hide-and-seek, and he was enjoying himself!

But Eddy stopped short when he glanced into the living room. He was stunned! Nothing could have prepared him for the sight before him. Double-D was equally surprised when came up and saw what Eddy was staring at.

"*Hmm*," Eddy said to Double-D. "And I thought *you* had problems." There, sitting at a tea table, was Ed.

He was wearing . . . *women's clothing!*

"*Quick, run away!*" Ed warned them.

Double-D and Eddy cracked up laughing. They couldn't help it. Ed looked so silly in his frilly dress and girlie chiffon hat.

Ed was the tallest of the Eds, and also the strongest. But Ed wasn't very smart. In fact, Eddy often wondered which was smarter, Ed or a bag of hammers? Now, looking at Ed in women's clothing, Eddy decided that the hammers were smarter, hands down.

"Don't fool around! Run!" Ed's eyes stared out from underneath the single eyebrow that stretched across his forehead.

"Excuse me, ma'am. Can Ed come out and play?" Eddy guffawed, ignoring Ed's warnings. Although he was usually cautious, Double-D didn't stop laughing, either.

Unfortunately, by this point it was too late. They were caught mid-giggle. A figure appeared between them, carrying dresses, and snarled in a loud, obnoxious voice, "Hey! No one can join my tea party without dressing up! So put on these dresses or leave."

It was Sarah, Ed's little sister. She was of small stature and very big mouth. Eddy was sure that if he looked up "spoiled brat" in the dictionary, Sarah's face would be pictured there.

"Forget it, Sarah," Eddy scoffed. No way was he going to dress up like a girl.

"*Grrrr!*" Sarah growled at her big brother and his friends.

"Huh?" Ed thought she seemed even scarier dressed as she was, like a queen. She even wore a royal crown.

Sarah yelled, "Tell your stupid friends it's *my* way or the *high*way!" Then she took in a deep breath and held it, her cheeks puffing out like two big pink balloons.

"Good luck," smiled Eddy. He couldn't believe Sarah would resort to such a childish game just to get them to wear dresses.

"Sarah! Stop it!" Ed ordered.

"Look, she's changing colors!" Eddy pointed. Sarah went from normal to red, to yellow, to green, to blue.

"Please, Eddy, she's gonna blow up," Ed pleaded, as Sarah turned a royal shade of purple.

Eddy didn't think she would blow up. He grew impatient with her nonsense and poked at one of her ballooned cheeks. "Cut it out, Sarah."

"Eddy, just put on the dress," Ed begged.

"No way, Ed!"

Tears were running down Sarah's swollen face.

"*Ahhh!* She's *leaking*, Eddy!" Ed cried. "Sarah, don't blow up!"

This was all too much. If Sarah did explode, Eddy knew he would be blamed. "All right! All right! I'll wear the stinking . . ."

"Here ya go!" Sarah said instantly, smiling happily and holding out a blue and white polka-dot dress.

4.

Soon, all three Eds were in dresses and silly hats, and were sitting at the royal tea table.

Sarah was ready to hold court. "I'm the queen and you are my servants. Now . . ."

"Smashing hat, Eddy," Ed interrupted, trying to play along.

"*Grrrr!*" Sarah growled at her big brother. "As I was saying, I am the queen!"

Ed nodded. "And we are your serviettes."

Eddy scowled. "Next thing you know, she's gonna want a throne."

Well, now that Eddy mentioned it, Sarah *did* want a throne. They had to stop the tea party to build one for her. Before long, Sarah was sitting on a beach chair, stacked high atop a bread basket, a kitchen chair, and a bar stool.

Thinking they'd done a pretty good job at throne

building, Eddy leaned back in his chair and raised his tea cup high. "A toast to my big mouth!"

Ding-dong! The doorbell rang.

The ringing surprised Eddy mid-toast, and he fell backward onto the floor.

"Get the door!" Queen Sarah screeched.

With a sigh, Eddy got up. It had turned into a really rotten afternoon. When he opened the door, it got even worse.

"It is I, Prince Jimmy!" said the visitor. He was dressed head to toe in a costume of princely finery — that is, if you didn't count the dental headgear that circled his head like a satellite orbiting the Earth.

Jimmy drove Eddy crazy. There wasn't anything wrong with Jimmy, really. He liked poetry and painting, dance and theater. He was mild-mannered. He was beginning to read great literature and was considered a sensitive sort. Yes, young Jimmy was a boy the girls could really talk to about the finer things in life.

That was more than enough for Eddy to brand him a wimpy loser.

Bang! Eddy welcomed Prince Jimmy by slamming the door in his face.

"Sheesh!" exclaimed Eddy. Things were going from absurd to absurder.

"Who was it?" demanded Sarah as Eddy returned.

"The frog prince," Eddy answered.

Ding-dong, ding-dong! Jimmy rang the bell again. He wasn't giving up a royal tea party that easily.

"*Grrr!*" Queen Sarah snarled at Eddy.

Ed jumped into service, "I'll get it, my queen!"

He fetched Jimmy and led him back into the living room, treating him like real nobility. Eddy smirked at this.

"Presenting the honor-a-po-pal Prince Jimmy!"

"Prince Jimmy has arrived!" Sarah was delighted. "Let the games begin!"

"Oh, goody, games!" Jimmy clapped daintily.

"Games? What games?" Double-D had a bad feeling about that.

Now it was Eddy who growled. "*Grrr.*"

5.

Apparently, they were going to have a race. A starting line was drawn on the floor. Ed and Eddy were fitted with racing bits, bridles, and reins. They got down on all fours.

As Prince Jimmy climbed atop his back, Ed declared, "I am a horse!"

Sarah yelled at Eddy from where she sat on his back, "Hey! You better win!"

From somewhere, Double-D produced a horn and trumpeted the start of the race.

"Go!" urged Sarah, kicking Eddy hard in the ribs.

Eddy took off like a shot, leaving Ed and Jimmy  in his dust. It took a moment for Ed to grasp that the race had begun. Jimmy and Double-D looked at him curiously.

"*Neigh!*" Ed finally realized what he was supposed to do, reared up, and jumped right into the race. Determined to win, he took off like a thunderbolt.

"*Whoa!*" cried Jimmy. Ed ran so fast, Jimmy wasn't riding him so much as hanging on for dear life.

Eddy flew down the hallway, with Ed in hot pursuit. By the time they reached the first turn, Ed had jumped into the lead.

"Go faster!" Sarah cried.

In the front room, Ed galloped over the couch. Jimmy clutched the reins tightly as he flew above Ed. With grim determination on his face, Ed leapt over a chair and zoomed up the staircase. Jimmy was dragged behind Ed, his face hitting every stair on the way up. *Bonk! Bonk! Bonk! Bonk!*

Eddy tried to close the gap as they sped up the stairs. It didn't help that Sarah was tugging on his tongue so hard, his tonsils were threatening to dislodge.

"Faster! Faster!" yelled Sarah.

Ed made a quick circle around the upstairs hallway and headed back down the staircase. Eddy followed on his heels and was catching up. As they headed into the home stretch, Eddy really poured on the speed!

It was neck and neck as they approached the wire.

They sprinted!

They huffed and puffed!

They jumped at the finish line, skidding across the floor with their arms stretched out in front of them!

It was close, just like a photo finish.

Of course, Ed was taller and his arms were longer. He crossed the finish line first.

Double-D dropped the black-and-white checkered flag with a flourish. "Prince Jimmy has won!"

"You lost, horsey!" scowled Sarah, as she repeatedly poked Eddy's head. "Bad! Bad! Bad! Bad! Bad!"

Eddy had had enough. He took off his bridle gear and threw it angrily.

"This stinks!"

Such impudence! Sarah didn't think a queen should have to put up with servants like Eddy. She wasn't going to take it anymore.

"To the dungeon with him!" she roared, as Jimmy snickered.

Eddy shivered, pretending to be deathly afraid. "The dungeon? Oh, no! I'm *so* scared," he said sarcastically, then laughed heartily at his own joke.

Not one to let someone else have the last laugh, Sarah pulled on a jump rope that hung from above and smiled. "Bye-bye!" she cried.

An upside-down playpen dropped from the ceiling. *Crash!* Eddy was helplessly trapped inside.

He wasn't laughing anymore.

6.

"Ed!" Eddy gripped the bars of his playpen prison. "Get me out! Ed! Double-D!"

Sarah, meanwhile, went on to other queenlike business. "Bring me my fool!" she ordered from atop her lofty throne. Prince Jimmy now had a throne of his own, right next to his queen.

"Okay," Ed said agreeably. After all, every proper queen had a good jester. Plus, he had an idea of how to get Eddy out of the slammer. It was one of his more amazing ideas, mainly because Ed had so few ideas to begin with. He leaned back as if he were doing the limbo and hurried over to Eddy's cage. He chuckled as he went.

Eddy was growling mad. "Spoiled brat. *Grrr.*"

"Please, Eddy, play along," Ed said as he lifted the playpen off Eddy with one hand. "Here's the fool!"

"No way!" Eddy groused.

Ed crammed a jester's hat onto Eddy's head.

"Eddy's a great fool, aren't you, Eddy?" Ed smiled, put a crushing arm around Eddy and gave him a thumbs-up sign.

"I said no!" Eddy was defiant.

"Bad baby-sitter!" Sarah screamed from her throne. "I'm telling Mom you left me all alone!"

"But then I won't get paid!" Ed said pitifully, bowing down before Sarah.

"Did you say 'paid'? You're getting PAID?" Eddy's tune suddenly changed. "I'm here for you, pal!"

 Eddy was now acting chummy with Ed. He'd do just about anything, if money was involved. Act like a fool? Why, yes, of course! All he needed was Double-D to blow his entrance music on the horn.

Dah toot toot, dah toot toot toot!

"This is fun!" cheered Jimmy in his princely outfit. Now he had a bandage on his forehead, thanks to the horse race.

With a big grin on his face, Eddy began his jester's act. "I just flew in from Peach Creek, and boy . . . "

" . . . are you stupid!" Sarah interrupted with a bored frown. She polished her nails.

"Yeah?" Eddy tried again. "So, why did the chicken cross the road?"

"To lay an egg, like you did just now!" Sarah sneered, before giving a big yawn.

Desperately, Eddy pulled out a dummy. It looked just like him, except it had bent nails driven into its head as hair.

"Say, Eddo, what's a ghost's favorite lunch meat?" Eddy asked his puppet.

He strained to answer in a high-pitched puppet voice, without moving his lips. "*Boo*-loney!"

"*Hrrrr!*" Sarah leaned down from her throne and yelled in Eddy's face. "You stink!"

Eddy couldn't believe it. He leaned over and whispered to Ed and

Double-D. "She has no taste! I used all my best stuff."

Ed was really getting nervous. "Don't give up now, Eddy!"

Ed threw Eddy back in front of the angry queen.

"Well?!" Sarah demanded.

Smiling brightly, Eddy pulled out a black top hat, the kind magicians use. He stirred around inside the hat with his hand. He then sat the hat on the floor and pulled with all his might. From the hat, he pulled Double-D out by his beanie.

Tah-dah! They both smiled. It was actually a pretty good trick.

Spoiled Sarah responded by hitting Eddy in the face with a tomato. Talk about a tough audience!

7.

Things were looking pretty desperate for Ed. If he didn't amuse Sarah soon, she would rat him out to their mom. Then he wouldn't get any cash to buy jawbreakers with!

"Here, Eddy, juggle this stuff!" Ed handed Eddy items from the room. "I'll get more."

Eddy held an end table, vase, football, cinderblock, book, teddy bear, bowling ball, toaster, cereal bowl, lamp, and bowling pin.

"More?" asked Eddy. It was going to be hard enough juggling what he had already. He threw the stuff into the air and started juggling. He was pretty good at it, too.

Prince Jimmy clapped excitedly. "Ooh, juggling!"

Unfortunately, Queen Sarah was unimpressed. "Boring!" she declared.

Ed's solution was to add more things to what Eddy was juggling. He picked up a card table and threw it. "Here, Eddy! Juggle this, too!" Ed volunteered.

"Oh, no!" Eddy cried.

Next, Ed threw in a stuffed chair. Then a television, canoe, aquarium (fish included), baseball, and refrigerator. Then he threw in Double-D.

Eddy was displaying an amazing amount of juggling talent. He managed to keep all the items in the air, circling 'round and 'round. But unfortunately, Ed pushed their luck just a little too far.

Ed threw in a cactus.

Of course, the cactus landed in Eddy's hand needles first.

"*AAAAAARRGH!*" Eddy screamed. He fell onto the floor as the needles sunk painfully into his palm. The stuff Eddy had been juggling dropped out of the air and crashed all around him.

Sarah laughed while Ed caught the stuffed chair before it hit the ground. The card table, however, hit Eddy square on the noggin.

Apparently, this was the kind of entertainment Sarah liked — the kind where things get broken and people get injured. She cackled louder and louder as Ed ran here and there catching the television and then the toaster.

"Oh, no!" Ed cried, grabbing the aquarium out of the air while Sarah chortled merrily.

The canoe landed on top of Eddy, finally dislodging the cactus from his hand. He pulled the canoe off and started to yell at Sarah, "Ah, shut —"

The refrigerator slammed down on him. *Smash!* Eddy opened the refrigerator door and stepped out.

Sarah was beside herself with glee. "That's more like it!" she squealed. Jimmy joined in and they laughed and laughed!

Sarah didn't want the destruction to end, so she reached down and picked up a vase.

Ed was angry. "Sarah! Don't throw stuff!"

Of course, she threw it anyway. Right at Ed's face.

"I got it!" Eddy yelled. He did get the vase, right after it hit Ed.

Then, Sarah threw a lamp. Ed jumped over the bowling ball and deftly caught the lamp before it hit the ground. In those two seconds, Ed managed to forget about the bowling ball behind him, tripped over it, and went splat.

As Jimmy joined in and tossed a teddy bear, Sarah continued slinging whatever she could reach from her perch atop the throne.

"I've got it!" Eddy tried to catch an end table, but it hit him in the head.

"I've got it!" Double-D tried to catch the beach chair, but it closed on him like a big clam.

"Double-D?" Ed went to his friend's rescue, opening the beach chair.

"Hello!" Double-D smiled from inside.

The beach chair snapped closed like a mousetrap on Ed's hand.

"*Ouch!*" Ed cried, waving his arm with the man-eating chair attached to it. He accidentally smacked

Eddy on the top of his head. "It wasn't me!" Ed fibbed unconvincing, as Eddy glared at him.

"Come on, Jimmy!" Sarah decided it was time for a more hands-on approach.

They jumped down from their thrones and proceeded to run around the house, picking things up and flinging them. "*Wheeee!*"

Miraculously, Ed, Edd, and Eddy were able to catch stuff before it broke, but it was pandemonium!

"Grab her!"

"There she goes!"

"*Whee!*"

"Sarah!"

"Get her, Double-D!"

"Sarah!"

"*Yay!*"

"SARAH!"

Things got wilder. Jimmy rode around on top of a vacuum cleaner with wheels. Sarah carefully aimed the bowling ball at the Eds and rolled it. "Fore!" she hollered.

27

Then she grabbed Jimmy from the vacuum and ran away as fast as she could.

"Sarah! No bowling in the house!" Ed chased after her, but found the bowling ball underfoot again. He had to run in place to avoid falling off the spinning ball.

"Whoa!"

The runaway vacuum cleaner rammed into Ed. Trying to get his footing, he accidentally turned the vacuum on. He was trapped riding it around while its powerful nozzle looked for something to suck in.

"Ed!" Eddy tried to rescue his friend but tripped over the pesky bowling ball and landed flat on his back.

"Eddy, the vase!" Double-D jumped on Eddy's belly to catch a flying vase.

"Get off of me!" Eddy yelled.

At that point, Ed and the vacuum cleaner smacked into them. They found themselves and the vacuum all balancing atop the bowling ball. Eddy was trying to keep them upright . . . with his tongue!

The powerful vacuum nozzle sucked in the bowling ball, then found Eddy's tongue, and slurped it right up!

Then it sucked in the rest of Eddy!

Then it sucked Ed in!

Then Double-D!

Then the vase that Double-D dropped!

Finally, the vacuum snatched up a big painting Sarah had thrown. Unfortunately, the painting was too much for the vacuum. It vibrated and wheezed, and pulled in more and more air, until . . .

KA-BLAMMO!

When the dust cleared, the Eds found themselves lying on the living room floor. They saw that everything in the living room had been either crushed, smashed, or torn asunder by the force of the vacuum's explosion. There was debris everywhere, plaster peeled from the walls, and a broken pipe leaked onto the carpet.

"Wow," Eddy murmured in the sudden quiet. "What a dump."

8.

Meanwhile, Sarah and Jimmy were still running around the house, wrecking things.

"We've gotta stop them!" Ed cried. He was going to be in huge trouble when his mom got home.

"Think, Eddy, think," Eddy told himself, trying to come up with a plan to catch the wayward brats. Suddenly, it came to him.

"Bingo!" He smiled.

Moments later, Sarah and Jimmy were having a pillow fight in one of the bedrooms, with feathers flying everywhere, when they heard something unexpected.

"All hail the great King Eddy!" announced Double-D.

Eddy sat on Sarah's throne as Ed crowned him. "Thanks, squire."

Sarah flew into the room, furious. "King?! There is no king! I'm *queen*!"

She grabbed Double-D and threw him to the floor. Eddy just smiled.

"Yeah, right." Eddy pulled on a jump rope attached to the upside-down playpen, which was once more hanging from the ceiling. *Crash!* It slammed down over Sarah, trapping her.

"My queen!" Jimmy was wide-eyed. He fled into another room and hid in a dresser drawer.

"I am the queen!" Sarah bellowed.

Eddy was getting a lot of satisfaction from this. "You're a squirt."

Ed, on the other hand, was so upset that he was slapping himself in the face. "Oh, no! Oh, no! My mom's gonna kill me. We gotta do something!"

It was true. Stopping Sarah was only half the battle. There was still a destroyed living room to deal with. What were they going to do?

Double-D smiled and raised a finger, "I have a suggestion!"

As time passed, Double-D and Ed created their

work of art. Double-D used a thin brush, painting delicate lines. Ed used a wide brush, spreading paint with broad strokes — most of which he got on himself.

"How's it going?" Eddy cruised in, examining their masterpiece. "Oooh, nice work! It's perfect!"

The Eds laughed at their cleverness. Eddy accidentally got wet paint all over his hand when he touched Ed. He wiped his hand on Ed's face.

"Let's set 'er up!" Eddy suggested.

Ed agreed, "Yeah! Let's do it!"

They hadn't tried to clean Ed's messy living room at all. There was still smashed, bashed, and ruined stuff all over the place.

Instead, Ed and Double-D had painted a crude portrait of a clean living room with sticklike versions of themselves standing around happily. They placed the painting near the front door, so Ed's mom would see it from the front door, first thing when she got home.

"There, all clean and fixed," Eddy laughed. "Your mom will never know!"

1.

It didn't take much to amuse Ed.

Ed was fascinated by a bright red yo-yo. He didn't actually know how to use a yo-yo very well, but that didn't affect his level of amusement. Most of the time, he would just let the string unwind while the yo-yo clanked to the ground.

"Boy, I'm good!" he twirled the yo-yo over his head like a lasso in Eddy's kitchen. "Yo-yo, yo-yo, yo-yo!"

Meanwhile, Eddy and Double-D prepared to make omelets. They ignored Ed's yo-yoing, because cooking was a very serious matter.

"Just as I thought," Double-D said, his nose in a cookbook. He carefully scooped some butter with a spoon and offered it to Eddy. "One teaspoon of butter, perfectly measured. Eddy?"

Without looking, Eddy grabbed the whole stick of butter, instead of Double-D's teaspoon worth.

"Fine, Double-D." Eddy grinned, slopping the butter into a hot pan. "You guys haven't lived until you've tried one of my omelets."

Eddy flipped the huge slab of butter several times in the pan, melting it. Then he took a shaker and sprinkled salt into the pan.

"Ed, eggs!" Eddy commanded. "I need eggs!"

Taking his focus off the yo-yo for a moment, Ed jumped into action. "I got 'em, Eddy!"

Unfortunately, the yo-yo was still swinging around Ed's head. The yo-yo's string wound tighter and tighter around Ed until he was all tied up. He fell face-first onto the kitchen floor. *Pow!*

Ed laughed and stood up, the yo-yo string still wound around him. "Almost there, Eddy!"

Ed tried to take another step and hit the floor again. *Pow!*

"Ed, you're denting the floor!" said Double-D.

Ed was on his feet again. "Oh, no way, Double-D! Not since I got my braces removed."

Now the yo-yo string was wrapped around only one of Ed's arms. He wriggled his arm this way and that, trying to dislodge it.

At the stove, Eddy was getting impatient. "Eggs, Ed, *eggs!*"

For some reason Ed walked over and checked inside the freezer. "Eggs, eggs, eggs, eggs, eggs, eggs, eggs . . . pop freeze!"

He didn't find any eggs there, but he did spot an old popsicle, out of its wrapper. Right away, Ed put his tongue on it for a taste.

"You won't find eggs in the freezer, monobrow!" Eddy frowned, still tipping the salt shaker until a small mountain of salt overflowed from the pan. "Look in the fridge, next to the milk."

Ed's tongue was stuck to the popsicle in the freezer. He turned to Eddy, stretching his tongue out further. "I'll be right back, Eddy!"

He opened the refrigerator's lower door, stuck his head in, and searched. He threw out all sorts of other food as he looked around. Finally, Ed emerged from the fridge with a tray filled with two dozen eggs.

"I found some eggs!" he cried.

"Bring 'em over," Eddy said. "I'm starving!"

"I'm Ed," Ed replied, running toward his friends.

Unfortunately, Ed's tongue was still stuck to the popsicle in the freezer. As he ran, he pulled the whole fridge over! It fell right on top of Ed's tongue, stopping him in his tracks. The eggs, however, kept going.

It was like an attack! Eddy held up his pan as the eggs pelted him, cracking and oozing yolk everywhere. The force of the egg assault knocked Eddy to the ground, which left Double-D as an open target. The rest of the eggs knocked Double-D over, too, and he joined Eddy on the slimy floor.

All the eggs were ruined. Eddy picked up his skillet again and walked toward Ed. "Ed? Oh, Ed?"

Ed had freed his tasty popsicle from the freezer,

but his tongue was still stretched *way* beyond normal. "Banana flavor, Eddy. Wanna bite?"

"Hold that thought," Eddy said, then smacked Ed in the face with his skillet. *Wham!*

"No eggs, no omelets, Eddy," Double-D said sadly. He squeezed yolk from his wet wool beanie.

"If we had a chicken, we'd be knee-deep in eggs." Eddy stopped wiping egg off his shirt and out of his hair. "A chicken! That's it!"

Unfortunately, Eddy forgot one of the most important rules to follow as a friend of Ed's: Never mention chickens around him without wearing football padding.

"A chicken?" Ed cried, tackling Eddy and smashing him to the floor.

He started jumping up and down on Eddy's belly. "Oh, please Eddy, can we get a chicken? Come on, Eddy! Oh, please, Eddy? Let's get a chicken! Can we, please?"

"Ooh! Ahh!" was all Eddy could say.

Finally, Ed stopped jumping and looked Eddy in the face. "I love chickens, Eddy!"

"Sure, Ed, you can have a chicken." Eddy smiled craftily. "But *I* get to keep the eggs."

2.

Rolf was busy tending his farm, so he had no idea his chores would soon be interrupted by the Eds. He lifted a hen from her nest and felt around under her.

"The hay is warm and tells Rolf all!" he proclaimed, pulling out a big egg. "*Ahh!* The fat has been trimmed and I will sleep well!"

Rolf held the hen close and looked into her eyes. "A fine egg. Rolf will remember!"

Suddenly, a commotion came from a nearby fence. Rolf was somewhat disappointed to see the Eds climbing over and through it.

"Look, chickens!" Ed said excitedly.

"And they lay eggs!" Eddy said happily, holding his hands out to Rolf, as if to play catch. "Hey, Rolf! Fire over that egg-maker!"

Ed ran around and tried to catch a chicken. "Chickens are fast!" he called as he chased one across the yard.

"Come on, Rolf, give us a chicken," Eddy asked. He said it nicely, as if giving away chickens was the most natural thing in the world.

Ed walked up with a smile and an armload of chickens.

"Has your brain turned to custardlike, half-priced pastry, Ed-boy?" Rolf looked at Eddy as if he were crazy. "I give you *no chicken!*"

Disappointed, Ed dropped his chicken-booty.

"It is very simple, like yourself, to hatch *your own* fowl," Rolf explained, as he pointed at his newly gathered egg.

Double-D rubbed his chin and smiled.

"*Hmm!* An opportunity to nurture the life and future of a domestic fowl seems appealing."

Ed sidled up to Rolf. "Where do eggs come from, Rolf?"

Before Rolf could respond, Double-D interrupted. "Eggs come from chickens, Ed."

"Where does a chicken come from?" Ed asked.

"An *egg*, slowpoke Ed!" Rolf took his egg and headed to his house. "My day is half-over, and you are half-full. Good-bye!"

"Wait! Rolf!" Eddy ran after him. "How 'bout that egg?"

Eddy grabbed for the egg, but Rolf was too fast for him. He snatched it away before Eddy could get his hands on it.

"You must *trade* for the egg, greasy Ed-boy," Rolf said, smiling.

"Trade? For what?"

"Sawdust," Rolf said, holding the tantalizing egg just out of Eddy's reach. "You want this egg, yes Ed-boy?"

3.

Rather than try to find sawdust to trade to Rolf, the Eds decided to make some. They found a big log and a saw, and prepared to cut.

"We'll have a chicken in no time," Eddy said, holding his sawdust-collecting cup and funnel.

"I love chickens, Eddy!" Ed exclaimed for the hundredth time.

Ed was tall enough to take one end of the saw, but Double-D had to reach way up to grab his end.

"The sawdust collector is ready." Eddy sat under the log with his cup and funnel. "Let's go, boys!"

Ed sawed with great gusto. All Double-D could do was hang on. He kept slamming painfully into the log.

Although he wasn't really doing anything, Eddy complained, "I'd hate to do this for a living."

"Stop! Stop sawing that log!" Jonny 2x4 ran up, yelling at them. As usual, Jonny carried his "best friend,"

Plank. It seemed Jonny and Plank were very much against the sawing of wood.

"But how are we supposed to get sawdust?" Eddy asked. "Maybe Plank would like to contribute?"

"Oh, no!" Jonny's glare disappeared as he listened to Plank "talk" to him. "Plank says that Kevin has lots of sawdust!"

"Kevin's got sawdust?!" Eddy threw his cup and funnel away, and ran right over Jonny on his way to Kevin's house. "Remind me to thank you later!"

"I'm getting a chicken," Ed told the now-dizzy Jonny as he ran by.

Kevin was grumpily doing chores, which meant throwing out a lot of sawdust.

"Sawdust stinks," Kevin glowered as he wiped the sweat from his brow. "Doing chores stinks."

It was a perfect situation for everyone involved: Kevin wanted to get rid of the sawdust without having to do any work; the Eds needed sawdust to trade with Rolf, and they were willing to haul it away free of charge. Double-D was sure it would be an easy transaction, if handled delicately.

"Excuse me, Kevin?" Double-D began as the Eds walked up. "We would like to offer our services and help you dispose of that . . ."

"Give us your sawdust, Kevin!" Eddy interrupted eagerly, then tried to downplay how important the sawdust was to them. "I mean, sawdust is so heavy, and it's always lying around doing nothing. Useless dust . . . from a saw, eh?"

"And our respect for wood byproducts will ensure it will be distributed to a loving home," Double-D said, trying to appeal to Kevin's charitable side.

"Fine, you can have the sawdust." Kevin sneered.

"Yeah! Now we can get my egg!" cheered Eddy.

Ed laughed. "And I can hug a chicken!"

But just then, Kevin added, "I'll trade you for ... painting my shed."

Kevin's shed was old, cracked, and needed painting in the worst way. The Eds were taken aback.

"Trade, schmade!" Eddy said angrily. "Paint your own lousy shed!"

"No sweat," Kevin moved the sawdust bin back toward the shed. "I'll just take this sawdust, and ..."

"No, wait!" cried Eddy desperately. "Um, so where's the paint?"

"What paint?" Kevin asked.

"How do we paint the shed without paint?"

Kevin smiled and walked away. "You figure it out ... dork!"

4.

Meanwhile, Jimmy was in his living room, painting a still life of some fruit in a bowl. He was making progress, but not without some minor annoyances.

"*Hmm!* Darn waxy buildup," Jimmy complained, as he polished a piece of fruit to a fine luster. "Perfect!"

He ran back to his canvas and continued painting.

"You're a pretty doll," he mumbled to himself as he worked, then looked back at the fruit bowl. "Huh?"

The Eds were inside his house, next to his fruit bowl! In fact, Eddy was posing on the table, with the fruit bowl on his back. "How's it going, Rembrandt?" Eddy asked.

Ed snacked on a piece of Jimmy's fruit.

"My painting is ruined!" Jimmy cried.

But Jimmy knew better than to hang around when the Eds showed up unexpectedly. He grabbed his paints, ran into a closet, and locked the door.

"Jimmy, wait!" Eddy tugged at the closet door. "Just give us some paint! Jimmy! Come on!"

Eddy tried twice to break the door down with his shoulder. Then he got smart and used Ed's head as a battering ram. But that didn't work, either!

"How much must an artist suffer? Oh, the torment," Jimmy moaned from the closet.

"Come out here, will ya?" Eddy stuck his hand under the door, feeling around. "We just need some lousy paint."

Jimmy squealed from inside the closet.

"Where are you, ya little . . . ?" Eddy reached in further, then jumped back with his hand painfully swollen and throbbing. "*Yeow!* He bit me! He bit me! Jimmy bit me! Jimmy bit me!"

"A starving artist, I suppose." Double-D laughed at his own joke. "I couldn't resist."

The Eds were in need of some diplomacy. Double-D

knocked politely on Jimmy's closet door. "Pardon me, Jimmy, perhaps we could interest you in a trade?" he asked.

"A trade?" Jimmy considered for a moment. "Clams!"

"Clams?" Double-D asked. It wasn't what he'd expected Jimmy to ask for.

Eddy approached the closet door angrily. "Clams?! Where the heck do you get ... ?"

Jimmy slammed open the closet door, smashing Eddy against the wall. He said, "No clams, no paint."

So the Eds left Jimmy's house, with Eddy grumbling, "Clams? What's with clams?"

They didn't know where to look for clams, so they rang every doorbell in the cul-de-sac.

Ding-dong!

"Could you spare some clams?" Eddy asked.

"No!"

Ding-dong!

"Pardon me, you wouldn't happen to have any

clams, would you?" asked Double-D.

"Nope!"

Ding-dong!

"Say, you haven't seen any clams around here, have you?" Eddy inquired.

"No, sir!"

Ding-dong!

"Could we borrow a cup of clams?" Double-D implored.

"No, nada, nix. Zero, zip, zilch on the clams."

Ed rang another doorbell.

Ding-dong!

"Can Eddy come out to play?"

"I'm right beside you, Ed," Eddy said.

Ed grinned. "Hi, Eddy!"

Just when things looked hopeless, Jonny and Plank appeared out of a manhole in the street, dripping wet. They each wore scuba gear, and Jonny was carrying a bucket full of . . . *clams!*

"Boy, Plank, you're hard to beat when it comes to gathering clams!" Jonny remarked.

"Clams?" Double-D asked.

Eddy grinned. "The clam master has arrived!"

"My, how convenient," Double-D scratched his head, bewildered.

"Just what we're looking for," Eddy said. "Toss a few of those clams our way, Jonny-boy."

"Trade ya, Eddy," Jonny said slyly.

Eddy's shoulders slumped in disappointment. "Sure, why not?" he asked, deflated.

Jonny smiled. "We'd like an anchor."

"An anchor? What are you, nuts?!" This was all too much for Eddy. "I'm going home!"

Eddy turned and took a few angry steps toward home. And then he yelled, "*Yaaah!*"

Eddy fell through the manhole and into the cold water below. Only Ed spoke as they all looked down at him, and he said the last thing Eddy wanted to hear. "But, I love chickens, Eddy!"

5.

The thing was, Eddy knew *exactly* where to get an anchor. But that meant having to deal with the three worst girls on the planet . . . the Kanker Sisters!

The Kanker Sisters were loud and obnoxious. The Kanker Sisters giggled and flirted with the Eds all the time. Worst of all, the Kanker Sisters were guaranteed to give you cooties! They lived in a trailer park not far from the cul-de-sac, where *no one* ever went.

The Eds had to use stealth if they wanted something from the Kanker Sisters.

When a tall stranger in a long  overcoat walked up to their door, the Kanker Sisters were busy giggling over an issue of *Tire Iron Weekly.* Behind them, hanging on the wall, was an anchor.

The tall stranger rang the buzzer.

Buzzzzzzz!

"Visitors!" the sisters squealed, and immediately started fighting about who would be the one to answer the door.

"Out of the way!" cried Lee Kanker. The red mop of hair on her head was so curly and thick, you couldn't even see her eyes.

"How's a knuckle sandwich sound?" Marie Kanker warned her sisters. She had blue hair and yellow teeth.

"Back off, dorks!" yelled blonde May Kanker, whose overbite was as big as the great outdoors.

Finally, Marie Kanker wrestled the door open.

The sisters ogled the tall stranger on their doorstep. His wide-brimmed, feathered hat was *so* out of fashion, and his sunglasses were ugly.

"Greetings, ladies," the stranger said. "Um, we're doing a survey and . . ."

A sound came from under the stranger's coat, which sounded strangely like, "Eddy!"

"Oh, uh . . . *ahem!* I mean, *I'm* doing a survey, and . . . ," the stranger now spoke in a deeper voice.

"Our mom's not home." Lee Kanker crossed her arms defiantly.

"Yeah, take a hike," Marie Kanker said rudely.

All three sisters cackled at this.

But the stranger didn't give up. "I was wondering . . . how many anchors do you own?"

"That's stupid!" said May Kanker.

Lee Kanker got up into the stranger's face. "You look familiar, mister."

The stranger stepped away, a bit off balance. The sound of chuckling came from under his long coat.

"Huh? Stop it, will ya?!" the stranger said, narrowing his eyes at Lee Kanker.

"You been on an infomercial?" asked May Kanker.

The stranger was by now sweating bullets. "Um, no . . . yes . . . I'm very well-known. Want my autograph?"

Just then, Ed stuck his head out through the buttons of the long coat. "I'm the legs," he said, laughing at how silly he sounded.

Eddy, who'd been the head of the stranger, fell backward onto the ground, taking the long coat down with him.

Double-D was riding on Ed's shoulders, where he'd been working the arms of the coat. "Oh, my! Exposed."

"It's our boyfriends!" Marie Kanker shouted happily, now recognizing them.

Lee Kanker smiled through her discolored teeth. "Eddy's such a weasel."

"Group hug! Let's kiss them!" Marie Kanker suggested, and the three sisters approached the boys with lips puckered, making smacking noises.

"Oh, no! Not me!" Ed cried. He took off running, with Double-D on his shoulders, dragging the coat behind them with Eddy still inside it.

The Kanker Sisters lunged with their lips, but missed.

"Run, Ed! Run!" Eddy hollered, and the Eds disappeared from the trailer park at top speed.

6.

Since the Eds couldn't get an anchor, Jonny said Plank would trade clams for a badminton racket. It just so happened that Ed's little sister, Sarah, and her friend Nazz were playing badminton nearby.

Sarah went to serve, only to find Eddy holding on to the end of her racket.

"Hey!" Sarah yelled.

"Give me your racket, Sarah," Eddy said.

"My serve!" Sarah responded by hitting Eddy with the racket. He bounced off the badminton net and crashed through a fence.

"Don't *ever* touch my racket!" Sarah warned.

"Sarah, we need it to trade for a chicken," Ed explained. "Please?"

"I'll trade you for a giant teddy bear," Sarah said sweetly.

"When will it end?!" Eddy cried.

They went back to Jimmy's, since everybody knew he had the biggest teddy bear in the cul-de-sac. He told them he'd trade his teddy bear for some plums.

"*Grrr!*" Eddy growled. "What's with the food?"

"Plums are good for you, Eddy," Double-D said sensibly.

It just so happened, Rolf had plums in his garden.

"So, back again, wanting Rolf's plums, confused Ed-boys?" Rolf was picking plums and putting them into a sack. "Do you not want my egg?"

"Yes, we want the egg!" Eddy was very frustrated. "But we need these plums first!"

Eddy tried to grab the sack of plums, but Rolf's grip was like iron.

"No plums, as I am still waiting for my sawdust! Do not fool Rolf!"

"Oh, I know! Let's trade!" Eddy searched his own

pockets. "How 'bout a nice comb for those plums?" he said, trying to make the comb look appealing.

"I have many, thank you." Rolf replied.

"I should have noticed," Eddy pulled a book from Double-D's pocket. "Let's see ... uh, how about this *Condensed Matter for the Advanced* book?"

Rolf wasn't going for it. Eddy pulled an abacus out of Double-D's pocket.

"Okay, okay! Uh, uh . . . ," Eddy didn't know what it was.

"Not my abacus, Eddy," Double-D said.

"I got a yo-yo," Ed let his bright red yo-yo unwind to the ground. "That move I just did is called 'Walking the Dog.'"

"It's over, Double-D," Eddy whined. "No egg, no chicken, no omelet."

Then they heard Rolf laughing.

"It is so simple, I am enjoying myself!" Rolf was playing with the yo-yo.

Eddy could only dare to hope. "Yo-yo for plums, Rolf?"

"Yes, Ed-boy," Rolf smiled and spun the yo-yo. "I have never seen such a thing. My family will sit around the stove telling stories of produce, bread, and Rolf's yo-yo for generations!"

And so the deal was struck. Rolf got the yo-yo, and the Eds got the sack of plums.

They traded Jimmy the sack of plums for his giant teddy bear.

They traded the teddy bear for Sarah's racket.

They traded the racket for Jonny's clams.

They traded clams for Jimmy's paint.

They painted Kevin's shack and got a barrel of sawdust.

They took the sawdust to Rolf.

"So, here's the sawdust," Eddy grinned. "Cough up the egg, Rolfie-boy!"

"Yes, the trade is complete!" nodded Rolf, holding up the egg. "Behold! Splendid!"

It *was* a splendid egg. It was big and it sparkled in the sunlight. Eddy was sure a fine chicken would hatch from it — one that would lay him many more eggs!

"It's mine!" Eddy grabbed the egg and held it like a newborn child, cradling it in his hands. "What I went through for you, baby."

"I'll begin drawing plans for an incubator," Double-D announced.

Ed gazed at the egg and smiled. "It has my eyes."

"And your thick outer shell," Eddy said.

"I want to hold it, Eddy!" Ed grabbed the egg from Eddy. "Oh! Let's play!"

"Ed! No, wait!" Eddy cried.

"You must be so cramped in there." Ed tapped on the egg. "Fly, chicken, fly!"

"No, Ed," Eddy pleaded. "You'll break it!"

Ed pulled at the opposite ends of the egg. The shell cracked open and yolk spilled to the ground.

"Uh, the chicken's gone bad," Ed said.

"Like my luck." Eddy could have broke down crying.

It was obvious to even the most casual observer that Edd, or "Double-D" as he was commonly known, was the most sensitive, intelligent, and thoughtful of the three Eds. He would spend hours in his room doing scientific experiments, thinking deep thoughts, and listening to classical music. Much like Jimmy, Double-D enjoyed reading and the arts.

Unlike Jimmy, however, Edd fit in well with Ed and Eddy. He had just the right amount of stamina and tolerance to put up with them. But it wasn't always easy.

Sometimes it was particularly hard, like the night that Ed, Edd, and Eddy spent camped out in a tent in Double-D's backyard. The whole cul-de-sac was going down to the creek the next day, and the Eds wanted to get up nice and early so they would be able to stake out the best spot.

Double-D thought they should kick back, relax, and turn in early. Ed and Eddy, however, were more interested in fighting over a big bag of potato chips.

"Ed! Quit hogging them!"

"Say 'pretty please,' Eddy!"

"In your dreams."

"Say 'pretty please with two eggs and a slice of bacon.'"

"Gimme the chips!"

Finally, Double-D got fed up and interrupted them. "Do you mind?" he snapped. "I'm trying to read."

"Don't read, just wait for the movie, Double-D," Eddy said. "Come on, Ed! I'm *starving*!" Eddy grabbed the bag and it tore open, sending chips flying everywhere.

"Oh, look at this, now!" Double-D complained. "Dried potatoes that may contain dextrose, salt, and saturated fats all over my sleeping bag!"

"Double-D made a mess in his sleeping bag, Ed!" Eddy joked. Ed laughed loudly at this (even though he didn't really get it).

"Hey, let's make a pie and hit me with it," Ed suggested out of the blue. This was his idea of a fun night! This or hugging chickens.

Eddy had other ideas. He turned on his flashlight and pointed it at Ed. A big shadow of Ed's head and torso was projected onto the tent wall. Eddy put his hand in the flashlight beam so that the silhouette of his hand looked like it was about to squeeze the shadow of Ed's head as if it were a nut.

"Doctor, I think we need to operate." Eddy grinned at Double-D.

Double-D forgot all about his messy sleeping bag and smiled. "Oh, I concur, doctor."

"Hold still, lumpy," Eddy said. He started "squeezing" Ed's shadow head with his shadow fingers. "Boink! Boink! Boink!"

"I feel it, Eddy!" Ed was amazed. "It's like voodoo."

Eddy and Double-D laughed.

"May I try?" Double-D put his fingers in the beam,

making the shadow of a perfect dinosaur skeleton on the tent. "Did you know shadow puppetry is one of the oldest forms of entertainment?"

"Like walnuts?" Ed asked. He tried to make a shadow puppet, too, jiggling his fingers in the light. All he could make was a silhouette of his hand. It wasn't very impressive. "Can you guess what it is?"

"*Hmmm.* Gee, Ed, is it a . . . hand?" Eddy smirked.

"*Oh! Oh!* Wait!" Ed tried again, and wiggling his fingers briskly, made . . . another hand. "I think it's broken, guys."

"What a lump!" Eddy laughed.

"Well, at least he's consistent," Double-D quipped. He and Eddy broke out laughing again.

"Excuse me," came a voice from outside. It was Jimmy, who lived next door. He opened his bedroom window to address the Eds, and he looked groggy and annoyed. "Do you mind? Some of us are trying to sleep," he grumbled.

"*Shh!*" Double-D whispered. "We're disturbing our neighbors, Eddy."

"Oh, are we?" Eddy said with an evil grin. He then proceeded to make rude noises with his armpit.

Blat! Blat-blat!

Ed found this hilarious. He and Eddy laughed loudly.

"*Shhh!* Eddy, please!" Double-D begged.

"Oh! Savages!" Jimmy angrily slammed his window.

Ed joined Eddy in making rude noises, and the laughing, *blats,* and *shh*-ing went on late into the night.

But eventually the Eds drifted off to sleep. They slept deeply and contentedly.

But when Eddy woke up the next morning, he came to an awful realization. "Wake up! We overslept!" he yelled, jumping up from his sleeping bag.

Eddy scrambled to get ready as Double-D shook his head. "Overslept?! Oh, dear, I've *never* overslept! I've blemished my personal résumé!"

"Ed, come on, wake up!" Eddy shook the still-snoozing Ed, who wore the chips bag on his head. "We've gotta get to the creek soon or we'll lose our spot at the swimming hole!"

In his sleepy haze (which just added to his usual haziness), Ed thought they had a dog named Spot that had gotten lost.

"Oh, no! Spot is lost!" Ed started running around, taking the tent with him. "Say it ain't so, Eddy!"

"Ed! This way!" Eddy cried. Then he turned to Double-D and said, "Hurry up, sockhead."

"But I haven't brushed my teeth, or had my crumpet, or . . . ," Double-D objected.

"Here, Spot! Come on, boy!" Ed was calling from up ahead.

"Ed, you're not listening." Now Double-D was following Eddy. "The *spot* by the creek."

"Spot's by the creek, Eddy!" yelled Ed.

"Tell me something I don't know!" Eddy replied.

As they ran, the boys quickly changed into their

swimsuits. That is, except for Ed. He wore his underpants when swimming, instead.

"Hi, Eddy!" pretty Nazz called out as the Eds passed. "Hi, Double-D."

"Hello, Ed," Ed added  helpfully.

"I see it! I see it!" Eddy's favorite spot by the creek was in the cool shade of a giant rock—and it was empty! "It's all ours! Oh, baby!"

But just as Eddy was about to stake his claim, Kevin came along and shoved him roughly into the water.

Splash!

Kevin smirked. "Didn't see you there, pal."

But the Eds knew darn well that Kevin *did* see Eddy, because the bully then took the best spot at the creek!

2

Eddy grabbed Kevin's leg and tried to pull him from the prime location. "That's *our* spot!" Eddy cried.

"I don't see your name on it, dork," Kevin smirked. He kicked, and Eddy went flying across the sand.

"I got him, Double-D, I got him!" Ed looked up in the air, stretched out his arms, and caught Eddy . . . sort of.

Eddy landed waist high in the sand. Ed was smashed into the sand, headfirst.

"Eddy, the swimming area's large enough to accommodate us all," Double-D said reasonably, pulling out his compass. "I'll just find you a better spot."

Eddy would have none of that. "No! Kevin *stole* our better spot!"

Meanwhile, Ed pulled his head out of the sand,

grabbed Eddy by the legs, and ran crying, "I got him, Double-D, I got him!"

A short while later, Ed, Edd, and Eddy were lounging in a new spot that Double-D had found for them. Eddy didn't like the new place at all! It was littered with trash, and there were chunks of rock everywhere. Worst of all, little flies were constantly buzzing around the Eds' heads.

"Nice spot, Double-D," Eddy remarked sarcastically. He sat up to reveal several rocks, a twig, and a soda can embedded in his backside. "Is there something on my back?"

"This isn't — ow — so bad, Eddy." Double-D tried to make the best of things. "Let's stay all day. *Ow!*"

Ed didn't mind their surroundings. He held two palm fronds so they stuck out of his neck. It made him look like a reptile. Every once in a while, he'd flick out his tongue at the passing flies. "Oink, oink, oink. Oink, oink, oink. I am a lizard."

Double-D chuckled and pulled a microscope out of his knapsack. "Well, Ed's lack of sleep is evident."

"This spot stinks!" Eddy kicked an old banana peel and shooed flies away. "There's rocks, garbage, and bugs everywhere!"

"Not to mention the lack of shade." Double-D removed a book, a bucket, and a vase from his sack. "Boy, is it *hot*!"

But Eddy was fed up. "Come on. Let's get out of here. I mean it."

"Oh, dear." Double-D dug around in the bottom of his knapsack and looked up in horror. "It can't be! I've forgotten my sunscreen!" he wailed. Double-D was not prone to emotional outbursts. But he had very fair skin, and just a few minutes in the sun could give him a terrible sunburn.

"I'm so vulnerable!" Double-D climbed into his knapsack and peeked out. "I can feel my flesh tighten . . . the stinging of the ultraviolet rays! Eddy! Kevin stole our spot!"

"Man, it's like a merry-go-round." Eddy was exasperated. "That's exactly what I said a couple of pages ago."

"But, Eddy, look at Kevin." Double-D's voice was full of envy. "He looks so comfortable."

Kevin chilled in the cool shade. He had a cold soda close at hand, and popped snacks into his mouth.

Eddy smirked. "Let's put a stamp on his head and mail him to Hollywood."

"Too inhumane, Eddy," Double-D replied.

Eddy saw that Double-D was glancing over at Jimmy and Sarah, who were making a sculpture in the sand. They had the spot right next to Kevin.

Double-D raised his eyebrows and explained, "In chess, to position oneself, one must first go through the pawns."

3.

Unaware they were being watched, Sarah and Jimmy built a sand sculpture that looked like a horse, with cucumber slices for eyes and seashells for ears. It also had a twig sticking out of its forehead.

"Unicorns are my specialty," Jimmy said proudly.

"It just needs a ribbon, Jimmy, and it'll be perfect," Sarah said. She left to find a ribbon.

As Jimmy admired his work, the unicorn began to vibrate and fall apart. Looking up, Jimmy saw Ed jumping up and down on top of it, trying to ride it!

"Look at me! Giddyap, you fat horse!" Ed cried.

"No, Ed! Stop!" Jimmy yelped. "Unicorns are sensitive!"

"Pshaw!" Ed replied, and pulled Jimmy atop the unicorn's back.

Jimmy still hadn't gotten over the *last* time he rode Ed like a horse. "Ed, my tummy! I feel queasy."

Ed kept riding on the sand sculpture until it no longer looked like a unicorn. By now, Jimmy was riding on Ed's back.

"Ed!" screamed Sarah, returning. "Put Jimmy down!"

Ed bucked Jimmy so he flew through the air and landed flat on his back. *Whump!*

At this point, Eddy decided to make his move, and he sauntered up to Jimmy. "Hi, Jimmy. Wanna play a different game?"

"Eddy?" Jimmy was still feeling a little dizzy.

Eddy grinned. "Ever play Splish-Splash in a Bath?" he asked Jimmy.

"*I* have!" Ed declared, stepping up to Eddy.

"Y-you have?" Eddy stammered.

Ed grabbed Eddy by the legs. "Splish-splash, take a bath!"

"Ed! Whoa!" Eddy yelled.

Ed threw Eddy into the creek with such force, he skipped across the water on his head four times! He slammed into a rotten, fungus-dripping tree on the edge of the creek. The tree and Eddy both fell into the water. *Sploosh!*

The skipping was so spectacular, Nazz and Rolf broke into applause from their nearby post on the sand.

"Bravo, Ed-boy!" Rolf said. "A fine toss!"

Ed was ecstatic. "I did a four-splasher . . . a new Splish-Splash record!"

Sarah pushed her big brother out of the way and headed for the creek. "Look out! I can beat your stupid record."

Jimmy followed, gingerly tiptoeing across the sand. "*Ow, eee, ha*, hot, *uh*, calluses!" he squealed.

"Excuse me, Jimmy," Double-D said as he cringed under an open book to protect himself from the sun.

"You wouldn't happen to have any more sunscreen, would you?"

Jimmy didn't, but just then Double-D was momentarily distracted from his sensitive skin problems. Eddy was taking Sarah and Jimmy's beach stuff and tossing it away from their spot.

"What are you waiting for, guys?" Eddy grinned. "Looks like those twerps have abandoned their spot. Now that we're in Sarah and Jimmy's spot, we're one small step away from kicking Kevin out of *our* spot."

"Ha!" Kevin snorted. "Good luck, beach blanket dorko!"

Kevin put his foot on an air pump and pushed down. His inflatable raft expanded rapidly as the air rushed into it. An ice-cold soda was sitting on the raft, and it suddenly flew into the air and landed upside down on Eddy's head. *Splurt!*

Ed pointed at the icy, overturned cola. "Are you going to finish that?" he asked.

"Give me back my spot, Kevin!" Eddy yelled.

"Hey!" Sarah had just returned, and she was mad. "Get out of our spot!"

Eddy had already prepared a clever retort. "Who is going to make us leave? You and what army?"

Uh-oh! Ed trembled and tried to shrink into himself. He knew it was not smart to taunt his little sister when she was angry.

Double-D tapped his fingers together nervously. "You'd think you would have learned by now, Eddy." But it was too late.

Sarah attacked.

As Jimmy watched, snickered, and stuck out his tongue, Sarah threw the Eds into the creek, skipping them across the water.

Splash! Splash! Splash! Splash! Splash!

"A new Splish-Splash record, indeed."

4.

Double-D's heretofore hidden floatation devices responded perfectly, and he was quickly brought back to the creek's surface. The lifesaver around his waist and the water wings at his shoulders kept him above water. After all, he was a great inventor!

"*Oooh!* That worked nicely." He smiled.

"Double-D, check it out!" Eddy pointed. "Our spot's empty!"

It was true. Sometime during their encounter with Sarah, Kevin had slipped away. The shady spot was alone and vulnerable.

Eddy grinned. "Let's grab it before—"

"I get back?" Suddenly, Kevin surfed by on his water raft and hopped back onto his beach towel in the shade. "*Heh heh!*"

"*Grrrr!*" Eddy was so angry, the creek water he stood in started to boil.

That reminded Double-D about his sensitive skin, and he nervously glanced at the sun. "Excuse me, Eddy, but I need to revisit the sun issue."

Eddy was not sympathetic. "You're like a broken record, Double-D. Geez!"

"Our being surrounded by water seems to be magnifying those ultraviolet rays I told you about earlier." Double-D pinched his increasingly pink arm flesh. "My skin's becoming quite sensitive, Eddy!"

"Yap, yap, yap," Eddy replied.

Then, instantly, the Eds were engulfed in a huge shadow.

"Look!" Double-D exclaimed. "It's an eclipse of the sun! Incredible!"

Oddly, it was Ed who knew the truth. "That's Jonny's head, Double-D."

Sure enough, when the other two squinted, they

could see Jonny sitting up on a flat, round rock on the hill next to the creek. The sun had moved in the afternoon sky, and now Jonny's head cast a shadow over the Eds in the creek.

"What's he doing up there?" Eddy asked, but then he had a sudden thought. "Hey, check it out! If we had Jonny's spot, we could keep an eye on *my* spot."

Indeed, the hill that Jonny and Plank sat on happened to be the very same one that cast the shade on Kevin's spot. From where Jonny was sitting, Eddy could easily spy on Kevin.

Double-D tried to cool down by fanning himself with his hand. "At that elevation, it must have a cooling cross breeze. Perhaps even shade," he noted.

"It's a cinch!" Eddy grinned and rubbed his hands together. He had a plan. "We just need to get rid of Jonny."

Ed's only contribution to the conversation was to pass gas underwater. Eddy and Double-D glared at Ed as stinky bubbles popped all around Ed's waist. Some help *he* was.

"Why couldn't you do that by Kevin?" Eddy asked.

5.

Soon, the Eds were climbing the hill up to where Jonny was sunbathing. Eddy rode Ed like a camel. In fact, as he climbed on all fours and grunted, Ed looked a lot like a camel.

As he rode, Eddy formulated a plan to get rid of Jonny. "Let's see . . . what do we need to get melonhead off his perch?" Eddy mused. "Explosives? Nah. A giant slingshot? Nope. A trapeze?"

He gasped. "Double-D, that's it!"

Double-D wasn't concerned with Eddy's plans. He was lagging behind, melting in the sweltering heat of an unforgiving sun. He couldn't care less about trapezes right then.

Eddy continued, "We'll use a trapeze. He'll never know what hit him! We'll lower some rope, and Ed, you can wear the tights."

"A bar mitzvah!" Ed concluded.

Eddy went on. "So, anyways, you just swing from over..."

"A trapeze?" Double-D interrupted angrily. "Please! Here's an idea, Eddy — next time, let's just sit in an oven!"

"Why don't you do something useful?" Eddy frowned at Double-D, "like, *hurry up!*"

Once they'd reached the top of the hill, Ed and Eddy peeked over the ledge at Jonny. Jonny was sunbathing with Plank at his side. He looked like he didn't have a care in the world.

"Pass me the trapeze, Ed," Eddy whispered.

"What?" Ed hadn't gotten the memo about the trapeze.

Double-D finally reached the top of the hill, behind his friends. Dripping with sweat, he passed Ed and Eddy, and walked over to where Jonny was basking in the sun.

"What's sockhead doing?" Eddy asked.

Double-D stood over Jonny and pulled out a silver whistle. He polished it, then blew it loudly.

Tweeeeeet!

Jonny immediately stood up, taking Plank in his hands. "I'm ready, coach!" he yelled.

Then Jonny trotted to the edge of the flat rock. He took a stance, bent at the knees, then jumped over the edge, taking Plank with him. After executing a near-perfect somersault, Jonny splashed into the creek.

Boosh!

Eddy was impressed. "Double-D, that was pure genius!" Now Jonny's spot on the rock was empty!

"Can we move on?" Double-D wiped the sweat from his brow. "This heat is unbearable."

Ed jumped on Jonny's sunscreen bottle with one foot, squirting a long flow of cream over the ledge. "The sound of a babbling brook makes me want to babble."

"Was that Jonny's sunscreen?!" Double-D felt sick. He needed that sunscreen!

Eddy crawled to the edge of the rock and looked

below. "Oh, this is perfect! Once Kevin moves, we'll just swoop in. We'll be kings of the swimming hole!"

"My kingdom for some sunscreen," Double-D sighed. He squeezed the bottle, but it was now empty. Just his luck.

"Ed, you be lookout," Eddy ordered.

"One, two, buckle my shoe," Ed said, then laid on the ledge and kept an eye out. For whom, he didn't know. Perhaps it was for their missing dog, Spot?

Eddy was proud of his battle strategy against Kevin. He plopped down on Jonny's beach towel. "Mess with me, will he?" Eddy mused.

For his part, Double-D just lay there, surrendering himself to his sizzling circumstances.

Time passed, until the sun lay low in the sky. Nazz left the creek, and Kevin followed.

From his lookout perch, Ed waved goodbye. "See ya, Kevin!" Ed called.

"Kevin left?" Eddy exclaimed, excited. "*Whoo-hoo!* Took him long enough. Slug."

Eddy had been playing with Jonny's large inflatable duck. Now he tossed it aside. It was time to gather up Double-D and head for the perfect spot, since it was finally empty.

"Assistance, please," came a small voice from the other end of the flat rock. "Assistance." It was Double-D.

Eddy went over to Double-D and looked down at him impatiently. "What's with you?"

"Mother Nature is so unforgiving," Double-D groaned. He was sunburned bright red, like a lobster, and couldn't move.

Ed chuckled, grabbed his arm, and lifted him to his feet. "Come on, Double-D."

"*Yeowch!*" Double-D hollered. "Don't touch me!"

Double-D was really upset. He walked around ranting, with his arms held straight out to his sides so they wouldn't touch the rest of his body. He looked like a bright red airplane!

"*Ow!* My face! Every nerve ending in the primary layers of my skin is screaming, 'Double-D, you nincompoop! You forgot the sunscreen!' *Yeeowch!*" Double-D was miserable.

Eddy tried to lighten the mood. "You look a little sunburned, Double-D," he noted.

"Don't toy with me, Eddy. I'll be peeling for weeks!"

"Welcome to the great outdoors, nature boy," Eddy scoffed. "What a whiner."

But when Eddy turned, they could see that half of *his* body was sunburned, too. In fact, there was a pale silhouette of his hand on his side, exactly where he'd rested his real hand as he sunbathed.

"I *am* a lizard," Ed chimed in. He, too, was sunburned on half his body. He poked his skin with a finger, and it turned from bright red to pink and back. "I changed colors. I have become . . . Chameleon Man! Oink!" Ed was quite pleased with himself. In his new role as Chameleon Man, Ed stepped up to Double-D with his index finger extended.

"Stay back!" Double-D cried as Ed poked his painful sunburn. "*Ouch!*"

"Oink!" Ed poked him again.

"*Ouch!* Eddy, make him stop!"

"Cut it out," Eddy said as he pulled Ed away from Double-D.

"Oink!" Ed poked Eddy on the top of his sunburned head.

"*Ow!*"

"You can be my sidekick, Frogmouth Kid!" Ed told Eddy. "And Double-D is our butler . . . um . . . Double-D!"

Eddy smacked Ed on the back.

"Oink!" Ed poked Eddy on his sunburned head again.

"*Yow!*"

"Oink!" Ed poked Double-D in the chest.

"Yeowch!"

"Oink!"

"Ouch!"

"Oink!"

"Ow!"

And that's the way Ed, Edd, and Eddy spent the rest of that sunny afternoon. Just another fun day at the creek!